Here's what kids have to say to
Mary Pope Osborne, author of
the Magic Tree House series:

*I have read every one of your books and I like
them so much that I even read them to my bird.*
—Ellie S.

*Your books are adventurous, exciting, spectacular,
and a whole list of other words.*—Alex W.

*When my teacher is reading, and when she has
to stop, the class says, "Mrs. Miller, one more
chapter, please."*—Kalais

*I love to write now. And now I know a lot more
about places and animals because I've read your
books.*—Brittney

*I will always keep these books, and I hope
someday to read them to my children.*
—Dennis D.

*When I can't make something, I don't just give up.
I think about Jack and Annie, and keep on going.*
—John

*Your books are excellent. Actually, they are more
than excellent. They are really, really excellent.*
—Kayla L.

Teachers and librarians love Magic Tree House books, too!

The children are skipping recesses just to read your books! In 25 years of teaching, I have never had such enthusiastic readers in my classroom. It is wonderful!—C. Kendziora

[The series] has been great in developing the children's understanding of story order and story elements. It has become a real catalyst in encouraging the children to write themselves. I thank you for the terrific job you have done in truly writing for children. You do this in a way that is inviting, exciting, as well as providing a glimpse of other times and places without patronizing young readers.—N. Roberts

An older cousin turned [my son] on to the Magic Tree House series, and the experience has turned him into a reading machine!
—A. Haroldson

We were astonished at [our son's] enthusiasm to read these books! He couldn't put them down and read till his eyes hurt.—R. Discenza

Thank you so much for writing books that children cannot put down, that teach them so much by "experiencing it," that spark a love of reading, that have them begging for more, and that have them reading while walking down the hall coming in from the bus! Thanks from the bottom of an old teacher's heart!—B. Taylo

I don't let my substitutes read the book [in the series] we're on to the class because I don't want to miss out on anything.—C. Todachinnie

We love Jack and Annie. We use our maps to find out where their latest adventure takes them. We have become scientists and take notes in science classes just like Jack does in the books. —J. Korinek

One of my students would refuse to read aloud in front of the class until I handed him his own Magic Tree House book. Now when we gather on the rug as a class, he is the first one who volunteers to read.—S. Stevens

Dear Readers,

I wrote this book because I've always loved the theater. When I was growing up, I performed in many plays. I even married an actor and playwright! My husband, Will, and I both love plays by Shakespeare. So for the past two summers, we've enjoyed visiting friends in England who put on plays by Shakespeare on the grounds of a castle. We also like to visit the replica of Shakespeare's Globe Theater in London.

My main research for <u>Stage Fright on a Summer Night</u>, though, comes from my memories of being onstage. Imagine waiting in the wings, heart pounding, palms sweating, knees shaking . . . Then you're on!

It's one of the most frightening and fun experiences you can think of. So I hope you'll be a little frightened and have a lot of fun when you share this adventure with Jack and Annie.

All my best,

Mary Pope Osborne

MAGIC TREE HOUSE® #25

Stage Fright
on a Summer Night

by Mary Pope Osborne

illustrated by Sal Murdocca

A STEPPING STONE BOOK™

Random House 🏠 New York

For James Simmons

Text copyright © 2002 by Mary Pope Osborne.
Illustrations copyright © 2002 by Sal Murdocca.

All rights reserved under International and Pan-American Copyright Conventions.
Published in the United States by Random House, Inc., New York, and
simultaneously in Canada by Random House of Canada Limited, Toronto.

www.randomhouse.com/magictreehouse

Library of Congress Cataloging-in-Publication Data
Osborne, Mary Pope.
Stage fright on a summer night / by Mary Pope Osborne ;
[Sal Murdocca, illustrator].
p. cm. — (Magic tree house ; #25)
SUMMARY: Jack and Annie travel in their magic tree house to Elizabethan London,
where they become actors in a production of *A Midsummer Night's Dream* and
try to rescue a tame bear.
ISBN 0-375-80611-3 (pbk. : alk. paper) — ISBN 0-375-90611-8 (lib. bdg.)
[1. Time travel—Fiction. 2. Theater—England—Fiction. 3. Magic—Fiction.
4. Tree houses—Fiction. 5. England—Fiction.] I. Murdocca, Sal, ill. II. Title.
PZ7.O81167 Ss 2002 [Fic]—dc21 2001048231

Printed in the United States of America   First Edition   March 2002
10 9 8

Random House, Inc. New York, Toronto, London, Sydney, Auckland

Contents

Prologue

One summer day in Frog Creek, Pennsylvania, a mysterious tree house appeared in the woods.

Eight-year-old Jack and his seven-year-old sister, Annie, climbed into the tree house. They found that it was filled with books.

Jack and Annie soon discovered that the tree house was magic. It could take them to the places in the books. All they had to do was point to a picture and wish to go there. While they are gone, no time at all passes in Frog Creek.

Along the way, Jack and Annie discovered that the tree house belongs to Morgan le Fay. Morgan is a magical librarian of Camelot, the long-ago kingdom of King Arthur. She travels through time and space, gathering books.

In Magic Tree House Books #5–8, Jack and Annie help free Morgan from a spell. In Books #9–12, they solve four ancient riddles and become Master Librarians.

In Magic Tree House Books #13–16, Jack and Annie have to save four ancient stories from being lost forever. In Magic Tree House Books #17–20, Jack and Annie free a mysterious little dog from a magic spell. In Magic Tree House Books #21–24, Jack and Annie help save Camelot. In Magic Tree House Books #25–28, Jack and Annie search for special kinds of magic.

1

Special Magic

Jack and Annie sat on their porch. Lightning bugs blinked in the warm summer twilight.

"Wow, a shooting star!" said Annie, pointing at the sky.

Jack looked up, just in time to see a streak of light flash through the sky. The light hovered above the Frog Creek woods. Then it disappeared into the treetops.

Jack caught his breath. He turned to Annie.

"That was no shooting star," he said.

"Right," she said.

They jumped up. Jack grabbed his backpack from inside the front hall.

"Dad, Mom! Can we go out?" he called. "We'll be back soon!"

"Ten minutes, no more!" their mom said.

"Okay!" said Jack. He closed the door. "Let's go! Hurry!"

He and Annie ran across their yard. They ran down their street. They ran into the woods. They ran until they came to the tallest oak. They looked up.

"Yep," said Annie.

Jack just smiled. He was too happy for words.

"That's our shooting star," said Annie. "The magic tree house."

She grabbed the rope ladder and started up. Jack followed.

When they climbed inside the tree house, they both gasped. A beautiful woman with long white hair stood in the shadowy corner.

"Hello, Jack and Annie," said Morgan le Fay.

"Morgan!" Jack and Annie cried.

They threw their arms around her.

"Why are you here?" said Annie. "What do you want us to do for you?"

"You have already done many good things for me," said Morgan, "and for King Arthur and Camelot. Now I want you to do something good for yourselves. You are going to learn magic."

"Oh, wow," said Annie. "Are we going to

become magicians? Will you teach us charms and spells?"

Morgan laughed. "There is magic that does not need charms or spells," she said. "You'll find a special magic on each of your next four adventures."

"How?" asked Jack.

"A secret rhyme will guide you on each journey," Morgan said. "Here this is the first." She held up a slip of paper.

Annie took the paper from Morgan and read the rhyme aloud:

To find a special magic,
You must step into the light
And without wand, spell, or charm,
Turn daytime into night.

"Turn daytime into night?" said Jack. "How can we do that?"

Morgan smiled.

6

"That's what you have to find out," she said.

Jack had lots of questions. But before he could ask any of them, a flash lit up the tree house. He closed his eyes against the light. When he opened them, Morgan le Fay was gone. On the floor where she had stood was a book.

"Morgan didn't tell us enough," said Jack.

"But she left this research book," said Annie. She picked up the book. "And it'll tell us the first place to go." She held the book up to the gray light at the window.

The cover showed a busy river with boats and a bridge. The title was

Merry Olde England

"What's o-l-d-e mean?" asked Annie.

"I think that's the old way of spelling *old*," said Jack. "You say it the same."

"So we're going to merry olde England to find magic?" said Annie. "That sounds fun. Ready?"

"I guess," said Jack. He still wished they'd gotten more information from Morgan. But he pointed at the cover of their research book.

"I wish we could go there," he said.

The wind started to blow.

The tree house started to spin.

The wind blew harder and harder.

Then everything was still.

Absolutely still.

2

London Bridge

Warm daylight flooded into the tree house. Jack opened his eyes.

Annie was wearing a long dress with an apron. Jack was wearing a shirt with puffy sleeves, knee-length pants, and tights. Their shoes were leather slippers. Jack's backpack was now a leather bag.

"These clothes are weird," said Jack. His voice was nearly drowned out by the sound of thundering wagon wheels coming from below.

"What's going on?" said Annie.

She and Jack looked out.

The tree house had landed in a patch of trees near a wide brown river. Wagons, carts, and people were heading toward the river.

Ferryboats, sailing ships, and white swans glided across the water.

"Wow, it's so busy," said Annie.

Jack opened their research book and read:

> In 1600, over 100,000 people lived in London, England. At that time, England was ruled by Queen Elizabeth the First. She was much loved by her people.

"A queen? Cool," said Annie.

Jack took out his notebook and wrote:

London—1600

Queen Elizabeth the First

"I've never seen a bridge like *that*," said Annie, looking to the left.

Jack looked with her. A giant stone bridge crossed the river. The bridge looked like a small town. It was crowded with houses, shops, and even a church.

Jack found a picture of the bridge in their research book. He read aloud:

> At the heart of London was London Bridge. The bridge crossed the Thames (say TEMZ) River. At different times in history, the bridge fell down. But it was always built again.

"Oh, wow," said Annie. "That must be where the song comes from." She sang, "London Bridge is falling down, falling down...."

While Annie sang, Jack took out his notebook and wrote:

London Bridge—crosses Thames (TEMZ)

River, crowded with stores and houses

"Let's go look for the magic," said Annie. She read Morgan's note again:

To find a special magic,
You must step into the light
And without wand, spell, or charm,
Turn daytime into night.

Jack squinted up at the sky. It was very blue, without even a cloud.

"It's just not possible," he said, shaking his head.

But he threw the research book and his notebook into his leather bag. Then he followed Annie down the rope ladder. When they reached the ground, they started walking toward the river.

"P-U!" Annie said, holding her nose.

The river smelled terrible.

No one else seemed to mind the smell, though. People were cheerfully piling into ferryboats or heading for the bridge. They all seemed happy, as if they were going someplace fun.

A group of ragged boys brushed past Jack and Annie. They were about twelve or thirteen years old. They were laughing and out of breath.

"Hurry! We'll be late!" one shouted.

The boys ran toward the stone gateway leading onto the bridge.

"Late for what?" said Annie. "What's on the other side of that bridge? Why are they in such a hurry to get there?"

"I don't know," said Jack. He pulled out their research book. "I'll see what the book says."

"No, let's just go—or *we'll* be late!" said Annie. She took off running.

"Okay, okay," said Jack.

He put away the book and ran after her toward London Bridge.

3

The Bear Garden

Jack and Annie passed under the stone gate-way that led onto London Bridge.

As they started across, Jack was amazed. The bridge was so noisy and smelly! Wagon wheels rumbled like thunder over the cobblestones. Pots clinked in carts. Horses neighed. Shopkeepers shouted.

"Good pies!"

"Hot peas!"

"New pins!"

"Shoes! Soap! Salt!"

A shopkeeper caught Jack's eye. "What lack you, boy?" he shouted.

"Nothing, thank you," said Jack, and kept walking.

"Watch out!" a cart driver yelled.

Jack grabbed Annie's hand. He pulled her out of the way. The cart rolled past them over the narrow roadway.

"Look!" said Annie. She pointed to a bear in a wooden cage in the back of the cart. The bear had matted brown fur. His head was down.

As the cart rumbled on, Jack shook his head. "What next?" he said.

"Them," said Annie, looking up.

She pointed at huge black birds sitting hunched at the edges of the rooftops. The birds sat still as they stared down at all the carts and animals and people crossing London Bridge. Jack shivered and moved quickly past the gaze of the giant silent birds.

Finally he and Annie came to the end of the bridge. They stepped onto the riverbank. There they stopped and looked around.

"I wonder where those big kids went," said Annie.

Jack studied the crowd heading down the road that led from the bridge. There was no sign of the group of ragged boys.

Jack took out their research book. He found the picture of London Bridge. He read aloud:

> **London Bridge connected London to the south bank of the river, an area where Londoners went for entertainment. The Bear Garden was a popular spot.**

"The Bear Garden?" said Annie. "That sounds good. Where's that?"

Jack found a map of the south bank. He pointed to a circle that was labeled BEAR GARDEN.

"Here," he said. He looked up. "And . . . *there*!" He pointed to a dark, round building in the distance.

"Great!" said Annie. "I want to see the garden filled with bears."

"Let's read—" started Jack.

"Let's *look*!" said Annie. She headed toward the Bear Garden.

Jack put away their book and followed her. As they got closer, they heard loud shouting and laughter coming from inside the round building.

Annie stopped.

"Wait," she said. "I'm getting a bad feeling about the Bear Garden. Maybe we *should* read more about it."

Jack opened their book again. He read aloud:

> At an arena called the Bear Garden,
> people watched bears fight with dogs.
> Animal fights were a common sport
> in old England. They are against the
> law today.

"Bears fight with dogs? Yuck!" said Annie. "I couldn't stand to watch that!"

"Me neither," said Jack. "Forget that place." He started to walk away.

"Hey, Jack! Look over there!" said Annie. She pointed to a cart nearby. "That's the bear that passed us on the bridge!"

4

A Midsummer Night's Dream

Annie and Jack ran over to the cart. In the back of it was a cage. In the cage was a big brown bear.

The bear was slumped over, his head still down. The sign on the cart said DAN THE DANCING BEAR.

"Dan?" Annie asked. "Are you going to fight?"

The lonely-looking bear raised his huge

head and looked at Annie. His dark eyes were sad. He let out a low moan.

"I understand," Annie said. "You don't want to fight. You're asking me to take you away." Annie reached for the door of the bear's cage.

"Away with you!" someone shouted angrily. "That's my bear!"

Jack and Annie whirled around. The cart driver was charging toward them.

"He's mine! I'm selling him!" the man shouted.

"Come on, Annie. Let's go," said Jack. He pulled her into the crowd walking down the road.

"But I have to save Dan!" said Annie, looking over her shoulder. "That guy wants to sell him to the bear fights!"

"I know," said Jack. "But we can't just steal him. That guy is his owner."

Jack looked around. He needed to get Annie's mind off the bear. He saw the group of older kids from the bridge. They were walking toward a round white building.

"Hey, look, the kids from the bridge!" he said. "Let's see where they're going."

"What about Dan?" said Annie.

"We can figure that out later," said Jack. "Let's follow those kids now."

He steered Annie toward the white building. When they got closer, Jack read the sign out front:

A PLAY AT THE GLOBE THEATER!

A MIDSUMMER NIGHT'S DREAM

Great! thought Jack. Annie loved plays. She loved acting in them at school.

A man stood at the door of the theater. He was holding a box.

"A penny to stand! A penny to stand!" he shouted.

The older kids dropped coins into the box and went inside.

"Wow, the play costs only a penny!" said Jack. "That's cheap!"

"But we don't have any pennies," said Annie. "Besides, I want to go back and free the bear."

Jack sighed.

"What will you do with him if you free him, Annie?" he asked.

"I'll figure something out," she said.

"Well, figure it out when the owner's not standing there," Jack said. "Right now, let's learn something about this *play*."

He quickly pulled out their research book. He found a picture of the Globe Theater. He wanted Annie to forget about the bear, so he read with lots of feeling:

> The first theaters were built in old England. Because there was *no* electricity, plays were performed during the day, when it was light. Almost *everyone* could afford to go.

"Neat, huh?" said Jack.

Annie sighed.

Jack kept reading in a loud, dramatic voice:

> Seating for the audience depended on how much was paid. The people who could afford the higher prices sat in galleries above the stage. Others stood in an area below the—

"Boy!" someone shouted.

Jack looked up.

A man hurried over to Jack and Annie. He was long-legged, with a trim beard and twinkly eyes.

"I could hear you from across the way," the man said. "You read very well!"

Jack smiled shyly.

"No, you are simply brilliant!" the man said. "And I am in *great* need of a boy who is a brilliant reader!"

5

Stage Fright

"Why do you need a boy who's a brilliant reader?" Annie asked the man.

"Because I have just lost two fairies!" he said. He pointed at Jack. "You can read both!"

And you are nuts, thought Jack. "Well, bye, see you around," he said. He nudged Annie to move along.

"Wait, wait," she said. She turned to the man. "What do you mean, my brother can read both fairies? Read them where?"

"Two boy actors didn't show up today to

28

play fairies," said the man. "But your brother reads with such expression! He can save us all!"

Jack stared. Was this guy saying what he thought he was saying?

"You mean you want Jack to be in your play?" said Annie.

"Indeed!" said the man. "There are three thousand people here today, waiting to see the play I have written! We cannot disappoint them, can we?"

"Three thousand?" said Jack.

"Yes!" said the man. "And one of them is the most important person in the world!"

"No. No way. I can't do that," said Jack. He had never liked being onstage. He always got stage fright.

"Wait, wait, Jack," said Annie. She turned to the man. "You need *two* fairies, right?"

"Yes," said the man.

"Well . . ." Annie tilted her head. Her voice went up. "I can read, too."

"Yes! Let Annie do it," said Jack. "She's a great reader. She can be *both* fairies!"

"Ah, but of course Annie cannot go onstage," the man said kindly.

"Why not?" asked Annie.

The man raised his eyebrows. "Surely you know it's against the law for girls to go on the stage," he said. "Boys must play all the girls' parts."

"But that's not fair!" said Annie.

"Indeed, 'tis not. But we cannot change the law now," said the man. He turned to Jack. "So, Jack? Will you join our players?"

"No thanks," said Jack. He tried to walk off, but Annie grabbed his arm.

"Wait, I think I know what Jack wants," she said to the man. "He will only be in your play if I can be in it, too."

"No, that's not what I want, Annie," Jack said under his breath.

"But, Jack, it would be so much fun," she whispered. "And there's nothing to be afraid of. You get to read your part. You don't have to memorize it."

Jack could tell that Annie really, *really* wanted to be in the play. And it was definitely a way to keep her mind off the bear.

"Uh, okay," he said, sighing. He looked at the man. "I'll be in your play—if Annie can be in it, too."

The man looked at Annie. She smiled eagerly at him.

The man smiled back.

"Why not?" he said. "But Annie will have to pretend to be a boy. She can tuck up her hair, and we'll call her Andy."

"Yay, thanks!" said Annie with a grin.

A trumpet blasted inside the theater.

"Hark, the play begins!" the man said. He took Jack and Annie by the hand.

"My name is Will, by the way," he said. "Come along, Jack and Andy! Be as swift as shadows!"

6

Onstage!

Will led Jack and Annie through a door into the back of the Globe Theater. Then he led them up a dark stairway.

As they headed upstairs, Jack heard laughter coming from the audience. His legs felt like jelly.

"This way," said Will.

He led Jack and Annie into a crowded, dimly lit room. Actors were rushing about everywhere. Each seemed to be in his own

33

world. One was pulling on a cape. Another was tying a rope around his waist. A third was whispering words to himself.

"I'll find your costumes," said Will.

As Will dug through a large basket of clothes, Jack and Annie looked around the costume room. It was crammed with fancy gowns, purple and blue capes, gold and silver wigs, stacks of hats, and masks.

"Cool," whispered Annie. She touched a donkey mask and a lion mask. "These would make good disguises, huh?"

Jack was amazed she was acting so calm. Didn't she know they were about to stand in front of three thousand people? The thought made him break into a sweat. His stomach felt fluttery.

"Here!" said Will. He handed them green

tunics, hats, and slippers. "Put these on! No time to dally! Your parts come up soon!"

Jack and Annie slipped behind a curtain and changed into their costumes. As they put on their hats, Annie hid her pigtails.

When they came out, Will handed them each a small scroll. "Here are your rolls," he said. "They have only *your* lines on them, no one else's."

Jack unrolled his scroll. He had two long speeches to read.

"Wait a second," he said. "I thought I just had a few lines. I didn't know I had a ton."

"Don't worry," said Will. "Just remember—speak very clearly and with feeling. And above all, act natural."

Act natural? thought Jack. *How do you*

act natural when you're about to have a heart attack?

Just then a short, chubby man burst into the costume room. He had curly hair and bright red cheeks. He was dressed all in green, too.

"For goodness' sakes, Will!" he said in a frantic whisper. "What will we do?"

"Don't worry! Look who I've found! They both can read!" said Will. He pushed Jack and Annie forward. "Jack and Andy, meet Puck, 'merry wanderer of the night.' He'll take you to the stage. Good luck!"

Annie smiled. Jack groaned.

"Come, boys!" said Puck. "Follow me!"

Puck led Jack and Annie out of the costume room into the hallway. Then he guided them to a dark area at the back of the stage.

Actors stood silently nearby, waiting to go on. One wore a beautiful white gown. Others wore tattered brown rags.

Through an arch, Jack saw the roof of the stage. It was blue with stars and a moon. A huge crowd stood directly in front of the stage. More people watched from the galleries above.

Every single person in England is out there! Jack thought with horror. *How did I let Annie talk me into this?*

"I'll take *you* onstage first," Puck whispered to Jack. "When I say, 'How now, spirit! Whither wander you?', start reading your lines. Understand?"

Jack barely nodded. His mouth felt dry. He tried to swallow, but he couldn't.

Puck turned to Annie.

"You go onstage with the fairy queen," he

whispered. He pointed to the actor dressed in the beautiful white gown. "When she tells you to sing her to sleep, you start your song."

"What's the tune?" asked Annie.

"Just make it up," said Puck. "Now, if they yell rude things, do not stop. Just—"

"If *who* yells rude things?" Jack broke in.

"The groundlings get a bit wild," said Puck.

"Groundlings?" said Jack.

"The rowdy folk who don't have seats," said Puck. "They're standing close to the stage. If they throw rotten fruit, don't stop, either. Just keep going."

That does it, thought Jack. He couldn't go onstage—not with groundlings throwing things, not with three thousand people watching, not with a million lines to read—and not when he was about to throw up!

While Puck and Annie watched the show, Jack slipped away. He looked for the exit. Just as he found the stairs, he bumped into Will.

"Where are you going?" Will whispered.

"I can't stay," said Jack. "I'm sick!"

Will sucked in his breath. But then he put his hands on Jack's shoulders and spoke calmly.

"Close your eyes for a moment, Jack," he said.

Jack closed his eyes. He could hear his heart pounding in his ears.

"There is nothing to fear," Will whispered. "Imagine you are a fairy. You're in the forest, on a summer night. See the silver moon overhead? Hear the owls? *Hooo-hooo*."

Will's deep whisper seemed to cast a spell

over Jack. He felt calmer. He could picture the silver moon. He could hear the hooting of the owls.

"Are you in the forest, on a summer night?" asked Will.

Jack nodded.

"If *you* believe that, the audience will believe it, too," whispered Will.

"We're on!" whispered Puck. The chubby actor ran to Jack. He grabbed his hand and pulled him along.

Before he knew it, Jack was onstage!

7

In the Forest, in the Night

Jack stood onstage in the bright sunlight. He felt three thousand pairs of eyes staring at him.

"How now, spirit!" Puck said in a loud voice. "Whither wander you?"

Jack looked down at his scroll. He pushed his glasses into place. He opened his mouth. No sound came out.

One of the groundlings hissed.

"How now, spirit!" Puck shouted even louder this time. "Whither wander you?"

Jack closed his eyes. He *felt* the summer night. He took a deep breath. He cleared his throat. He looked at his speech.

Then he began to read:

Over hill, over dale,
Through bush, through briar,
Over park, over pale,
Through flood, through fire,
I do wander everywhere,
Swifter than the moon's sphere;
And I serve the Fairy Queen. . . .

As Jack read, the audience grew quiet. Jack forgot he was Jack. He was in the forest, in the night, talking to Puck.

When he finished, not a single groundling hissed or threw things.

Jack took a deep breath as Puck started his lines. Jack knew he had one more speech. His heart pounded. But it was more from excitement now than fear.

When it was time to start his second speech, he was ready. This time, he spoke very clearly and with feeling. He tried to be as natural as possible. When he finished his speech, the audience clapped and clapped.

Jack hardly remembered leaving the stage. Will was waiting for him.

"Hurrah!" said Will, slapping Jack on the back. "You were brilliant!"

Jack blushed as he gave Will his scroll back. He couldn't believe he'd just performed, *acted*, in front of all those people! And he'd actually had fun—just like Annie had said.

Jack waited in the shadows for Annie to

do her part. He watched her go onstage with the fairy queen and the other fairies.

When the queen asked the fairies to sing her to sleep, Annie stepped forward. Reading from her scroll, she sang out clearly—and with *lots* of feeling:

You spotted snakes, with double tongue,
Thorny hedgehogs, be not seen;

Annie waved her hand as if shooing away the snakes and hedgehogs.

Newts and blind worms, do no wrong;
Come not near our Fairy Queen. . . .

Annie shook her finger at the newts and blind worms. The audience howled with laughter.

Annie kept singing. She made funny movements and silly faces to go with the words. She even added a little dance to her song.

By the time she finished, the audience clapped and cheered and stamped their feet.

"Wonderful, job, Andy!" Will said when Annie left the stage.

"You were brilliant!" Jack told her.

"Thanks!" said Annie. She gave her scroll back to Will. "Do I go on again?"

"Not until the end, when we all bow," said Will.

Just then Jack heard the audience laughing again. He really wanted to see the play. So he found a shadowy spot at the back of the theater and watched from there.

Jack couldn't understand everything people said, but he could understand the story. It was about people in love. But none were able to marry the people they loved.

The funniest part was about the fairy king and fairy queen. The king was mad at the queen. So he put magic juice on her eyelids to make her fall in love with the first person she saw.

Puck worked for the king. He wanted to make the king's trick even funnier. So he put the head of a donkey on a funny man. When the queen woke up, she saw the donkey-man. The magic made her fall madly in love with him!

The fairy king finally broke the spell. Puck turned the donkey-man back into a human while he slept. When the man woke up, he looked about in wonder.

"I have had a most rare vision," he said. "I have had a dream. . . ."

Jack whispered the words to himself. *"I have had a most rare vision. I have had a dream."*

Beside him, a group of actors gathered for the last scene of the play.

"My lion mask is missing!" one of them wailed. "I cannot be a lion without my mask!"

"Hush, of course you can," said Will. "Just roar! And roar again!"

Will pushed the actor onstage. He wiped his brow. Then he caught sight of Jack.

"Get Andy!" he said. "It's almost time for our bow."

Annie? Where is Annie? Jack wondered. He hadn't seen her in a while. He peeked into the costume room. She wasn't there.

Jack's heart started to pound. He had a scary thought. . . .

"Oh, no," he whispered.

Jack ran down the stairs. He opened the door. He was happy to see Annie running out from some trees behind the theater.

"It's time to bow!" he said, grabbing her hand. "Where have you been? What did you do?"

"I'll show you later!" said Annie.

Jack and Annie charged upstairs together.

They found Will and some of the actors waiting.

Puck was finishing his last speech onstage:

So good night unto you all.

Give me your hands if we be friends. . . .

"Andy! Jack!" said Will. He grabbed Annie and Jack.

Puck ended his speech. The audience gave a big hand. They clapped and whistled and shouted.

Jack and Annie ran onstage with Will and the other actors. While the crowd cheered, they all bowed once . . . twice . . . and once again.

8

The Most Important Person

Will stepped forward and held up his hands. Slowly the crowd quieted down.

"Thank you all," he said. "And thank you to the most important person in all the world. She has graced us with her presence today."

Will made a sweeping bow to a woman in a gallery above the stage. The woman wore a white dress with pearls. A veil covered her face.

The woman stood up and slowly lifted the veil. She had pale, wrinkled skin and small dark eyes. She wore a red wig.

The audience members let out a gasp. They all fell to their knees.

"Long live Queen Elizabeth!" said Will.

"Long live Queen Elizabeth!" the crowd shouted.

"Long live Queen Elizabeth!" shouted Jack and Annie.

The queen smiled. Her teeth were all black! The audience didn't seem to mind. They cheered even louder.

The queen raised one hand and the crowd instantly hushed.

"I thank you, my good people," she said. "And I thank all these good players, every one. Today, they gave us a special kind of magic—the magic of theater. They turned the very daytime into night."

"Oh, man," whispered Jack. That was it—the special magic. Their search was over.

The audience cheered again. When the actors left the stage, they gathered around Will to congratulate him on his success.

Annie pulled Jack aside.

"We found it!" she said. "The magic!"

"I know!" Jack said. "Will helped us. Let's thank him!"

"Later," said Annie. "First I have to show you something. I need your help! Quick!"

Annie led Jack downstairs and outside. As people streamed away from the Globe, the late afternoon sun was going down.

"This way," said Annie. She headed for the patch of trees behind the theater.

When she and Jack stepped into the gloomy shade, Jack saw an odd figure near a tree. A purple cape barely covered his furry back. A golden wig and a lion mask barely hid his furry head.

Jack gasped. "The bear! You stole him!"

"I *had* to," said Annie. "I went to the cart when no one was looking. I put a costume on him. So if we passed people on the way here, they'd think he was an actor."

"But you can't just steal him!" said Jack.

"I wasn't stealing. I was *saving*," said Annie. "I'm not sure what to do with him now. What do you think?"

Just then the bear's owner charged into the woods. "Where's my bear?" he shouted. His face was red. He was scowling.

"Thieves!" he yelled. "Give him back! I'm selling him to the fights!"

"NO!" said Annie, standing between the bear and the man. "He's a tame bear! Not a fighter!"

"She's right!" said Jack, jumping in. "And besides, bear fighting is stupid! Really stupid!"

"'Tis, indeed," said a deep voice.

Jack, Annie, and the bear's owner whirled around. Will and Puck were standing at the edge of the woods.

9

Sweet Sorrow

"Tut, tut, you're a sorry sight, man," Will said to the bear's owner. "Trying to sell an old tame bear to the fights. Well, I've been planning to write a play with a part for a bear. So take this money for him and be gone."

Will handed some gold coins to the bear's owner.

The man's eyes grew wide. He laughed.

"You can have him!" the man said. And he took off.

"Thank *you*, and good riddance!" called

57

Will. Then he turned to Puck. "Take our new player to the stables. Tell the actors they needn't be afraid of him. He's tamer than most of them."

"Come this way," Puck said. He put his arm around the bear and gently led him out from the trees. "You'll love the stage, old man."

"Bye, Puck! Bye, Dan!" said Annie.

Puck smiled and waved. The bear stared for a moment at Jack and Annie. He had a grateful look in his eyes. Then he lumbered off with Puck.

"Thanks, Will, for helping Dan," said Annie. "And for helping us."

"Thank you both for helping *me*," said Will. "You saved the day."

"The *night*, you mean," said Jack.

"Indeed, the night," said Will. "Oh, here is

your bag. You forgot it." He gave Jack his leather bag. Then he held up their two scrolls with their lines on them.

"And you can take these," said Will. He handed them to Jack, and Jack put them in his bag.

"Where are you off to now?" said Will.

"The other side of London Bridge," said Annie.

"Ah, I can take you there in my boat," said Will. "Follow me."

Will led them along a dusty path toward the river. The last rays of the sun slanted through the trees. Soon they came to a small rowboat docked on the Thames.

"Climb in," said Will.

Jack, Annie, and Will climbed in. Will untied the boat from the dock. Then he began rowing across the river.

The water reflected the purple and pink in the sky. Only a few white swans now glided over the shimmering ripples. The river smelled as bad as before, but Jack didn't mind now. He had grown used to it.

Jack pulled out his notebook and pencil.

"What are you doing?" Will asked.

"I wanted to write some of my memories in my notebook," said Jack.

"Ah, and I'll note you both in *my* book of memory," said Will.

Jack smiled.

"I have a question, Will," said Annie. "Why does Queen Elizabeth have black teeth?"

"Too much sugar," said Will.

"I hope it doesn't make her feel bad—looking that way, I mean," said Annie.

"Oh, no, she's not the least hurt," said Will. "The queen has no idea how she looks. She hasn't peeked in a good mirror for twenty years."

"Is that true?" said Annie.

"'Tis," said Will. "The queen pretends to be young and beautiful. Just as *you* pretended to be a boy, and the bear pretended to be an actor. You see, all the world's a stage."

Jack liked that idea. He wrote in his notebook:

All the world's a stage.

Jack looked up at London Bridge as they passed by. The shops on the bridge were closed now. The theater crowd was thinning out.

The scary black birds were no longer on

the rooftops. They had swooped down and were picking at the garbage left on the cobblestones.

The show was over.

By the time they came to the riverbank, night was falling. It was much cooler. Will tied up his rowboat and climbed ashore with Jack and Annie.

"Thanks a lot," Jack said to Will. "We can go the rest of the way by ourselves."

"Where do you live?" said Will.

"In Frog Creek," said Annie.

"What path do you take?" asked Will.

"You'll never believe this," said Annie. "We climb up the rope ladder to a tree house in that tree over there. And we open a book—"

"Then we make a wish," said Jack, "and we go to the place in the book."

Will smiled.

"Thy life's a miracle, isn't it?" he said.

"Yes!" said Annie. Jack nodded. He liked the way Will looked at things.

"I have an idea," said Will. "Why don't you both stay here instead? You can live and act at the Globe Theater. I'll ask the queen to exclude you from the law about girls going onstage, Annie—because of your great talent. And I will teach you both to write plays."

"Really?" said Jack and Annie together.

Jack couldn't imagine anything more fun. Then he thought of his parents back in Frog Creek.

"But our mom and dad—" he said.

"We would really miss them," said Annie.

Will smiled.

"I understand," he said. "And I would miss *you* if I were *them*." He put his hand over his heart. "So, good night, good night. Parting is such sweet sorrow."

"Yes, 'tis," said Annie, nodding.

"Farewell!" said Will. He waved.

Jack and Annie waved back. Then Will turned on his heels and headed back to his rowboat.

Jack and Annie walked to the rope ladder and climbed up to the tree house. When they got inside, they looked out the window.

Will was rowing back across the Thames River. A single white swan glided across the ripples beside his boat. A silver moon was rising in the sky.

At that moment, Jack *did* feel sweet

sorrow. He wanted to stay in merry olde England just a little longer.

"Wait, Will!" he shouted.

But Annie picked up the Pennsylvania book.

"I wish we could go home," she said.

The wind started to blow.

The tree house started to spin.

It spun faster and faster.

Then everything was still.

Absolutely still.

10

Our Will?

Jack opened his eyes.

They were wearing their own clothes again. A lightning bug blinked inside the growing darkness of the tree house.

Annie picked up Morgan's note. She repeated the rhyme:

To find a special magic,
You must step into the light
And without wand, spell, or charm,
Turn daytime into night.

"We found the special magic," said Annie. "Theater magic!"

"Yep," said Jack.

He opened his backpack. He and Annie took out the two scrolls Will had given them. When they unrolled them, Jack saw that Will had written something. He read aloud:

> Thank you both for helping me.
>
> Your friend,
> William Shakespeare

"William *Shakespeare*?" said Annie. "I've heard that name before."

"Me too," said Jack.

He took out their research book. He looked up *Shakespeare* in the index. He turned to a page and read aloud:

> William Shakespeare lived from 1564 to 1616. He wrote thirty-seven plays and many sonnets and other poems. Many people think he was the greatest writer who ever lived.

"The greatest?" said Annie. "*Our* Will?"

"Oh, man," whispered Jack. He stared in amazement at William Shakespeare's autograph.

"Hey, we can leave our scrolls with Morgan's note," said Annie. "It'll prove to her we found a special magic."

They put their two scrolls next to the note on the floor. Then they climbed down the rope ladder.

When they started walking through the woods, a breeze blew, shaking the tree leaves. Shadows shifted. Birds called from hidden places.

"Remember the enchanted woods?" Annie said in a hushed voice. "The fairy queen and the fairy king?"

Jack smiled and nodded.

"And Puck, the merry wanderer of the night?" said Annie. "And Will, *our* Will."

Jack nodded again.

"I had a great time," said Annie. "Didn't you?"

Jack sighed.

"Yes," he said. Then he took a deep breath and spoke very clearly and with feeling:

"I have had a most rare vision.
I have had a dream. . . ."

MORE FACTS FOR
JACK AND ANNIE AND *YOU*!

William Shakespeare *did* write a play that included a small part for a bear. That play is called *The Winter's Tale*.

Queen Elizabeth's teeth *were* black from eating too much sugar (as were the teeth of many other people from that time). One of the queen's ladies-in-waiting wrote that the queen was not given a clear mirror to look at herself for the last twenty years of her life.

There is no historical evidence that Queen Elizabeth I ever visited the Globe Theater. It is believed, though, that she liked Shakespeare's plays very much and that *A Midsummer Night's Dream* was performed at her palace for her and her court.

Today, the place where theaters sell tickets is called a "box office." That's because in Shakespeare's time, people dropped their admission money into a *box* held at the door.

The reason actors' parts are now called "roles" is because in Shakespeare's time, actors were given scrolls, or *rolls* of paper, with only their own lines written on them.

For over 400 years, people have been quoting lines written by Shakespeare. Some of the lines quoted in this book are:

"I'll note you in my book of memory."
—from *Henry the Sixth*

"All the world's a stage." —from *As You Like It*

"Good night, good night! Parting is such sweet sorrow." —from *Romeo and Juliet*

"Thy life's a miracle." —from *King Lear*

"I have had a most rare vision. I have had a dream past the wit of man to say what dream it was." —from *A Midsummer Night's Dream*

It is believed that William Shakespeare invented over 2,000 words and expressions, many of which we still use. Some of Shakespeare's words in this story are:

blushing	hush
bump	lonely
downstairs	long-legged
excitement	shooting star
for goodness' sakes	sorry sight
forward	swift as a shadow
gloomy	tut, tut
good riddance	upstairs
howled	

Are you a fan of the Magic Tree House series?
Then here's your chance to write your own
adventure with Jack and Annie.
Enter the Magic Tree House
Playwriting Contest!

Visit our

MAGIC TREE HOUSE®

Web site at

www.randomhouse.com/magictreehouse

The Magic Tree House Web site also has
exciting sneak previews of the next book,
games, puzzles, and lots of other fun activities!

Discover the facts
behind the fiction!

Do you love the *real* things you find
out in the Magic Tree House books?
Join Jack and Annie as they share all the
great research they've done about the
cool places they've been in the

MAGIC TREE HOUSE® RESEARCH GUIDES

The must-have companions for your favorite
Magic Tree House adventures!

Don't miss the next Magic Tree House book,
in which Jack and Annie visit an
African forest in the clouds . . .

MAGIC TREE HOUSE® #26

GOOD MORNING, GORILLAS

Where have *you* traveled in the

MAGIC TREE HOUSE®?

#1–4: The Mystery of the Tree House*

❑ **#1 DINOSAURS BEFORE DARK** Jack and Annie find the tree house and travel to the time of dinosaurs.

❑ **#2 THE KNIGHT AT DAWN** Jack and Annie go to the time of knights and explore a castle.

❑ **#3 MUMMIES IN THE MORNING** Jack and Annie go to ancient Egypt and get lost in a pyramid while helping a ghost queen.

❑ **#4 PIRATES PAST NOON** Jack and Annie travel back in time and meet pirates with a treasure map.

#5–8: The Mystery of the Magic Spell*

☐ **#5 NIGHT OF THE NINJAS** Jack and Annie go to old Japan and learn the secrets of the ninjas.

☐ **#6 AFTERNOON ON THE AMAZON** Jack and Annie go to the Amazon rain forest and are greeted by army ants, crocodiles, and flesh-eating piranhas.

☐ **#7 SUNSET OF THE SABERTOOTH** Jack and Annie go back to the Ice Age—the world of woolly mammoths, sabertooth tigers, and a mysterious sorcerer.

☐ **#8 MIDNIGHT ON THE MOON** Jack and Annie go *forward* in time and explore the moon.

#9–12: The Mystery of the Ancient Riddles*

☐ **#9 DOLPHINS AT DAYBREAK** Jack and Annie take a mini-submarine into the world of sharks and dolphins.

- ❑ **#10 GHOST TOWN AT SUNDOWN** Jack and Annie travel to the Wild West, where they battle horse thieves, meet a kindly cowboy, and get help from a ghost.
- ❑ **#11 LIONS AT LUNCHTIME** Jack and Annie go to the plains of Africa, where they help wild animals cross a rushing river and have a picnic with a Masai warrior.
- ❑ **#12 POLAR BEARS PAST BEDTIME** Jack and Annie go to the Arctic, where they meet a seal hunter, play with polar bear cubs, and get trapped on thin ice.

#13–16: The Mystery of the Lost Stories*

- ❑ **#13 VACATION UNDER THE VOLCANO** Jack and Annie land in Pompeii during Roman times, on the very day Mount Vesuvius erupts!
- ❑ **#14 DAY OF THE DRAGON KING** Jack and Annie travel back to ancient China, where they must face an emperor who burns books.

#21–24: The Mystery of Morgan's Library*

☐ **#21 CIVIL WAR ON SUNDAY** Jack and Annie go back in time to the War Between the States and help a famous nurse named Clara Barton.

☐ **#22 REVOLUTIONARY WAR ON WEDNESDAY** Jack and Annie go to the shores of the Delaware River the night George Washington and his troops prepare for their famous crossing!

☐ **#23 TWISTER ON TUESDAY** Jack and Annie help save students in a frontier schoolhouse when a tornado hits.

☐ **#24 EARTHQUAKE IN THE EARLY MORNING** Jack and Annie go to San Francisco in 1906—just as the famous earthquake is shaking things up!

Join Jack and Annie as they go on a quest
to save Camelot in a special hardcover
Magic Tree House® book!

A STEPPING STONE BOOK™

Great authors write great books . . .

Grades 1–3

Duz Shedd series
  by Marjorie Weinman Sharmat
Junie B. Jones series by Barbara Park
Magic Tree House® series
  by Mary Pope Osborne
Marvin Redpost series by Louis Sachar
Mole and Shrew series
  by Jackie French Koller

Clyde Robert Bulla
The Chalk Box Kid
The Paint Brush Kid
White Bird

Jerry Spinelli
Tooter Pepperday
Blue Ribbon Blues: A Tooter Tale

Grades 2–4

A to Z Mysteries® series by Ron Roy
The Katie Lynn Cookie Company series
  by G. E. Stanley
Zenon: Girl of the 21st Century series
  by Marilyn Sadler

**Stephanie Spinner &
Jonathan Etra**
Aliens for Breakfast
Aliens for Lunch
Aliens for Dinner

Gloria Whelan
Next Spring an Oriole
Silver
Hannah
Night of the Full Moon
Shadow of the Wolf

NONFICTION
Magic Tree House® **Research Guides**
  by Will Osborne and
  Mary Pope Osborne

Grades 3–5

The Magic Elements Quartet
  by Mallory Loehr
#1: Water Wishes
#2: Earth Magic
#3: Wind Spell
#4: Fire Dreams

Spider Kane Mysteries
  by Mary Pope Osborne
#1: Spider Kane and the Mystery Under
  the May-Apple
#2: Spider Kane and the Mystery at
  Jumbo Nightcrawler's

NONFICTION
Thomas Conklin
The *Titanic* Sinks!

Elizabeth Cody Kimmel
Balto and the Great Race

Look for these other books
by Mary Pope Osborne!

Picture books:
Kate and the Beanstalk
The Brave Little Seamstress
Moonhorse
Rocking Horse Christmas

For middle-grade readers:
Adaline Falling Star
American Tall Tales
The Deadly Power of Medusa
Favorite Greek Myths
Favorite Medieval Tales
Favorite Norse Myths
The Life of Jesus in Masterpieces of Art
Mermaid Tales from Around the World
My Brother's Keeper
My Secret War
One World, Many Religions
*Spider Kane and the Mystery Under
  the May-Apple (#1)*
*Spider Kane and the Mystery at
  Jumbo Nightcrawler's (#2)*
Standing in the Light

For young adult readers:
Haunted Waters